RODDY DOYLE

ROVER AND THE BIG FAT BABY

Illustrated by Chris Judge

MACMILLAN CHILDREN'S BOOKS

First published 2016 by Macmillan Children's Books

This edition published 2017 by Macmillan Children's Books
an imprint of Pan Macmillan
20 New Wharf Road, London N1 9RR
Associated companies throughout the world
www.panmacmillan.com

ISBN 978-1-5098-3686-4

1 3 5 7 9 8 6 4 2

A CIP catalogue record for this book is available from
the British Library.

Printed and bound by CPI Group (UK) Ltd, Croydon CR0 4YY

For Amy and Casey

Chapter One

Rover was asleep.

But, really, he was only pretending to be asleep. He closed his eyes and snored and farted.

Hey, pal!

Yes, Rover?

Too much information there.

OK. Sorry, Rover. I'll start again.

Rover was asleep.

But, really, he was only pretending to be asleep. Rover was actually awake.

Wide awake.

Because Rover never slept.

He liked to be sure that if anything happened,

he'd know all about it. Sometimes Rover knew about things even before they happened.

It was early in the morning and Rover had been up all night, delivering poo.

Rover was a business dog. Probably the most successful business dog in Ireland. He was quite old. In fact, Rover was very old. He was more than a hundred years old in dog years. And even older in wasp years. He'd been a leading business dog for almost twenty human years.

But the thing was – Rover's brain wasn't old. His legs and his tail had slowed down but his brain hadn't. His brain was wide awake and working twenty-four hours a day. So, Rover was still Ireland's most successful business dog. Although there was a dog in Wicklow called Cindy who was doing very well too.

Cindy chased sheepdogs away from the sheep, because the sheep paid her to do it. Wicklow is full of mountains and the mountains are covered in sheep. There are more sheep than people in Wicklow. And this is the big secret: sheep are more intelligent than people.

Really?

Is that you, Rover?

No, the reader.

Oh, someone's reading the book! How exciting!

Yeah, but, like, are sheep really brainier than people?

Yes.

Then how come they just stand on the sides of mountains and go, like, 'Baa'?

Good question. They stand on the sides of mountains and go 'Baa' because they want to.

But that's stupid.

Not really. Humans love to stand on the sides of mountains too. They pay lots of money to go all over the world, to countries like Peru and Canada, so they can climb up the sides of mountains and stand there. One of Rover's owners, Billie Jean Fleetwood-Mack, had climbed mountains in Argentina, Kenya and even a tiny mountain in Holland.

Yeah, but she didn't go 'Baa'.

That's true. But she wanted to. Years later, Billie Jean wished she'd gone, like, 'Baa'.

Back to the story.

Chapter Baa – Sorry, Chapter Two

Rover had been up all night, delivering poo. It was summertime and summer is always a busy time for the Gigglers.

Who are the Gigglers?

That's a good question. The Gigglers are small, furry creatures who look after kids and make sure that the grown-ups always treat them properly. But they do it so quietly that hardly anybody has ever seen them. The Gigglers hide themselves so well that hardly anybody knows that they even exist.

'Oh, look, there's a Giggler!'

'What's a Giggler?'

'Eh – I don't know.'

'Then how do you know that you saw one?'

'I don't know.'

'Then you probably didn't see one.'

'OK.'

'What was it you probably didn't see, again?'

'I can't remember.'

But just because the Gigglers are hardly ever seen doesn't mean they aren't there. Because they are. Wherever there is a child, there is a Giggler somewhere very near, looking after the child.

If an adult is mean to a child, he or she will get the Giggler Treatment. The Giggler Treatment is usually dog poo on the grown-up's shoe or, because it's summer in this story, the grown-up's sandal.

Or flip-flop.

The Gigglers keep giving the adult the Giggler

6

Treatment – that is, poo on the flip-flop – until the adult stops being mean to the child. And summer is like the Gigglers' Christmas. Because the kids are home from school and they drive their parents and guardians and minders and everybody over the age of twenty-five mad.

'You're driving me mad!'

Those were the most popular words spoken in Ireland during the months of July and August.

'You're driving me mad!'

They were music to the fluffy ears of the Gigglers. And Rover liked them too. When Rover heard those words – 'You're driving me mad!' – he sat back and thought, 'You're making me rich.'

The Gigglers needed a steady supply of top-quality poo and, as everybody knows, if you're looking for poo, a dog is your only man. It's quite amazing how much poo comes out of a dog. All dog lovers know this.

'Will you look at that poo!'

'What a dog! Good boy, Bonzo.'

Dogs are walking poo factories and they never shut down for the holidays. If the Gigglers needed

poo, the dogs of Dublin were there to deliver.
Or, more exactly, one dog in Dublin was there to
deliver. And that dog was Rover.

Most dogs are eejits. That's why we love them.
'Oh, look at the way Bonzo ran into that tree!'
'He's gas.'
But Bonzo isn't gas at all. He's just a dope.
He produced the poo but he hadn't a clue what
to do with it. He just left it on the path or in the
garden, and carried on chasing a wasp or a bee or
the shadow of his own tail. He had no idea how
valuable that poo was.
But Rover did.

Rover looked at dog poo and saw money.
The Gigglers needed a supply of dog poo. They
weren't dogs themselves and their own poo
wasn't suitable. In fact, Giggler poo wasn't really
poo at all. Because the Gigglers poo flowers.

No way.

It's true. The Gigglers poo flowers. The next
time you're at a wedding and you see the bride
walking up the aisle, carrying a lovely bright
bouquet of—

Giggler poo?

Exactly. Not all cut flowers are Giggler poo but
some of them are. The point is, Giggler poo isn't
suitable for the Giggler Treatment because no
grown-up is going to step on flowers and think
they are being punished. So, the Gigglers needed
a much pooier kind of poo.

Dog poo.

Correct. The Gigglers needed a steady and a
large supply of dog poo during the summer. The
kids were at home, driving everyone mad.

'You're driving me mad!'

'Me too!'

'You're driving us mad!"

'Me too!'

'You're driving *everyone* mad!!'

'Us too!'

There were mad adults all over Dublin being mean to children, and the Gigglers were run off their little feet trying to keep up.

'A dad is just after throwing his son's ice cream out the car window,' said the smallest Giggler.

'Why?' said the biggest Giggler.

'The son said it wasn't white enough.'

'That's no reason to throw it out the window.'

'Giggler Treatment?' the smallest asked.

'Giggler Treatment,' the biggest Giggler agreed. 'Text the order to Rover.'

She watched the smaller Giggler's fingers and thumbs thumping out the text on her gigPhone.

What's a gigPhone?

Use your imagination.

OK.

The smaller Giggler read out the text before she sent it.

'Seventeen poos, please, Rover. ASAP. And no hard ones. X.'

'Very good,' said the biggest Giggler.

'Activate?'

'Activate.'

'I love this bit,' said the smaller Giggler, and she pressed the 'send' button.

All the Gigglers went, 'Whoooosh!'

Excuse me . . .

Yes?

What does ASAP mean?

I don't have time to answer. But I will – as soon as possible. But now we have to dash on to a new chapter, to explain two very important things.

Is the Big Fat Baby one of the very important things?

No.

Chapter Three – Which Has Two Important Things … But No Baby

The first important thing was the time of year. It was summer, and people who own dogs know what the summer does to dog poo. The sun dries the poo and makes it hard. Even in Ireland, where the sun spends most its time hiding behind the clouds, the poo's only out of the dog a few minutes and it's already hard as a stone.

This was Rover's problem. He had to deliver fresh poo to the Gigglers. It had to be soft and horrible. It had to be very bad news for the grown-up who stood on it. But in the summer the poo wasn't fresh for very long. The Gigglers had just ordered seventeen dog poos. It was the middle of summer. So Rover had to be fast.

Rover needed help.

And this was the second important thing. Rover had help. He had an assistant. Batman had Robin, Shrek had Donkey, Sherlock Holmes had Watson. And Rover had Messi.

Messi was Rover's nephew.

Do dogs really have nephews?

Yes, they do – sometimes. Rover had a sister called Doris, and Doris had a lot of puppies.

How many?

A lot. Loads. A big number. Dublin was full of Rover's nieces and nephews. Rover loved them all but Messi was his favourite.

Why?

Good question. Messi was a very small dog but he was packed with questions and ideas and energy. And Rover loved that.

Why?

Because Messi reminded Rover of what Rover had been like when he was a pup.

How?

You're asking more questions than Messi. Are you Messi?

No.

Then stay quiet, please. I've a story to write and you have a story to read.

Now there's a third very important thing that I have to tell you about but it will have wait until the next chapter.

Is it about the Big Fat Baby?

No.

Chapter Four

Rover took off his reading glasses and put his phone back in the secret place where he always hid it. He had just read the latest text from the Gigglers.

'Seventeen poos,' he said. 'Come on, Messi.'

'Why, Uncle Rover?' asked Messi.

'We've got work to do.'

'OK, Uncle Rover,' said Messi. 'Just let me finish this.'

The two dogs were in the shed in the Macks' back garden. Rover used to live in the house next door. But he'd spent so much time with the Mack children – years before, when the children were little kids – that he'd moved into the Macks' shed. He'd become the Macks' dog. The Macks gave a box of biscuits to the neighbours, and the neighbours gave Rover to the Macks. Everyone was happy.

Hey, pal.

Yes, Rover?

They were chocolate biscuits.

Thanks, Rover.

Top of the range.

Thank you, Rover.

There was an old rug in the shed, and Messi's toys. The shed was also the centre of Rover's business empire.

Messi loved working with his Uncle Rover. But one thing annoyed him.

Mess.

The rug annoyed him because it was messy. It would never stay straight. It was dark brown and there were red tassels, just like long pieces of red wool, along two of its sides. And the long pieces of wool wouldn't stay in the right place for Messi. He spent hours trying to get all the wool bits to stay perfectly straight. He spent most of his life, all six months of it, running around the rug, trying to make crooked things behave like straight things. Because Messi was a very tidy pup.

'Come on, Messi,' said Rover. 'We have to go.'

'Nearly done, Uncle Rover,' said Messi. 'Oh, no.'

There were 502 tassels attached to the sides of the rug, and one of them – just one of them – was sticking up. But it shouldn't have been sticking up. Wool wasn't supposed to stick up in the air and annoy a little dog. But it did.

Messi fell over.

And that is the third important thing you need to know.

Messi had a tail.

Chapter Five
The Tale of Messi's Tail

Messi's tail was very—

Excuse me . . .

Yes?

Why did Rover hide his phone?

Good question – sort of. Have you ever seen a dog with a phone?

No.

And what would you do if you ever saw a dog talking into a phone?

I'd go, 'Holy cow, there's a dog with a better phone than mine, like.'

So, a dog using a phone is not something you would ever expect to see. If Rover was seen with his phone it would give the game away. Am I right?

Yes. I suppose so.

Can we move on with the story?

Yes, please.

Good – great. Off we go. Young Messi's tail was very long and the rest of Messi was very small. Really, Messi's tail was way too big for him. And nearly every time he wagged it, he fell over. Dogs wag their tails when they're happy and excited, and Messi was a happy dog and he was often very excited, even when he was annoyed. Messi really loved being annoyed. So he fell over quite a lot.

Like now.

Messi fell over just when Rover was trying to get him out of the shed. It was a lovely day out there and the sun was baking the poo. If they didn't hurry up, the poo would be so hard the Gigglers would claim that it wasn't poo at all and that Rover was trying to sell them stones. The Gigglers paid a euro for every poo but only if they were happy that it really was poo and not rocks pretending to be poo.

Excuse me . . .

Yes?

I am a rock.

Oh.

And I have never pretended to be a poo. And I think I speak on behalf of all rocks when I say that no rock has ever claimed to be a poo. We demand an apology.

Sorry.

A written apology.

It *is* written.

Oh yes, so it is. Carry on with the story. But hurry up. Or I'll throw myself through your granny's kitchen window.

Rover was in a hurry.

Messi stood up – and fell over again.

'Sorry, Uncle Rover.'

'Ah now, Messi,' said Rover.

Rover loved Messi. He loved teaching Messi all the tricks – how to be a top-class dog and how to become a top-secret business dog. One day soon, Messi was going to take over the business. But the kid's tail was getting in the way. For such a tidy dog, Messi's tail was very untidy.

Messi stood up – and stayed up.

'Good man, Messi,' said Rover. 'Now. Are you a tail with a dog or a dog with a tail?'

Messi thought about this.

'I'm a dog with a tail,' said Messi.

'Good man,' said Rover. 'And who's in charge? You or the tail?'

'Me,' said Messi.

'That's the right answer,' said Rover.

And Messi fell over. He always did when his Uncle Rover told him he was right.

'So,' said Rover. 'How are we going to make that tail of yours behave?'

'Don't know, Uncle Rover. How?'

'Well, here's an idea,' said Rover. 'Whenever you know your tail is going to wag, think of

something you don't like. Does that make sense, Messi?'

'Yes,' said Messi. 'That's a great idea, Uncle Rover.'

Rover grabbed Messi's tail, so Messi wouldn't collapse.

'So, what'll you think about?' asked Rover.

'Messy things,' said Messi. 'I don't like messy things.'

'OK,' said Rover. 'Let's give it try. Here we go. Ready?'

'Yes,' said Messi.

'Good man,' said Rover. 'Let's go, Messi! Time waits for no dog. Let's go trap some poo!'

And Messi stayed upright. Rover watched

Messi's super-serious face as he thought about mess and stopped his tail from wagging. It was an impressive sight. All that effort – it made Rover tired just looking at him. Messi was still up on his four little legs. Now they could go to work.

'Good man, Messi,' said Rover. 'Let's go.'

And Messi fell over.

But now he had an idea of his own.

'I'll say messy things out loud when my tail starts going fizzy,' he said.

'Good idea,' said Rover.

'Odd socks!' said Messi.

And he didn't fall over.

They ran out the door of the shed.

'Soggy cornflakes!' said Messi.

Chapter Six

The shed was in the Macks' back garden and
Rover needed fifteen portions of poo.

Excuse me . . .

Yes?

You said seventeen.

Yes, I did. But Rover already had two.

Where did he get them?

How many dogs are in this story?

Two.

There's your answer.

Rover and Messi needed to get from the back
garden to the front of the house. This was easy
because there was a narrow alley at the side of
the house. There was a high gate at the end of

the alley and it was locked. But Rover was a good jumper, and jumping on to the top of the wooden gate was easy.

Rover jumped now – and his front paws grabbed the top of the gate and he was able to pull himself up the rest of the way. He looked back down at Messi.

'Ready, Messi?'

'Dirty dishes!' said Messi.

And he jumped. His tail was wagging like mad but it didn't matter because he was in mid-air. He caught Rover and Rover caught him. He climbed up Rover's hind legs and back and sat on Rover's head.

'What's the view like up there, Messi?' asked Rover.

'It's a bit messy,' said Messi. 'Those mountains way over there look out of place.'

'Leave the mountains alone, Messi,' said Rover. 'They've been there for thousands of years.'

'Hmmmm,' said Messi.

'See any dogs?'

'Yes,' said Messi. 'Lots.'

'Great.'

'They're all going in different directions,' said Messi. 'They're very unorganized.'

'Great,' said Rover. 'Just remember this, Messi. Our business depends on messy dogs.'

'Hmmmmmmm,' said Messi.

He climbed down off Rover's head and sat beside Rover on top of the gate.

'Let's go,' said Rover.

'Wet towels!' said Messi.

Rover jumped down and Messi went right after him – and landed right on top of him.

Excuse me . . .

You're going to ask about the big fat baby.

Yes.

Don't worry. She's on her way.

Rover and Messi were now in the Macks' front garden. They ran to the front gate. Just as Missis Mack – that is, Billie Jean Fleetwood-Mack – got there. She'd been out running with the BFB.

A VERY SHORT HISTORY OF THE MACK FAMILY

Mister Mack met Billie Jean Fleetwood in a supermarket, called Super-Thing. She was looking at the high-energy biscuits and he was avoiding the cream crackers. They bumped into each other and got married.

In the supermarket?

Yes. It was love at first special offer.

They had three children.

Did they buy them in the supermarket?

No. They bought them on eBay.

Really?

No.

They had three children: two boys, called Robbie and Jimmy, and a girl called Kayla. The children grew up and became those things that most scientists call adults. Then—

OH NO!

A supermarket is a big shop that sells food and household goods, like toothpaste and nappies. Isn't that interesting?

A NOT-AS-SHORT-AS-I-THOUGHT-IT-WOULD-BE HISTORY OF THE MACK FAMILY
II

Then Robbie met a girl called Miriam Bigge.
They fell in love when they fell down a hole. They
were walking down a street in Dublin when there
was an earthquake. Dublin doesn't have many
earthquakes and this was only a little one. In fact,
it wasn't really an earthquake. An old water pipe

under the street broke and the paving right above it collapsed. It wasn't an earthquake at all.

But that's not the way things work in Dublin. If it rains for an hour, it's the heaviest rainfall of all time.

'I've never seen anything like it. The water came up to my chin!'

'The poor cat was swept away. He ended up in France!'

A strong wind becomes a tornado.

'I've never seen anything like it. It lifted the house!'

'It landed right beside the cat.'

Two motorbikes go roaring past.

'I've never seen anything like it. I thought we were being invaded by aliens.'

Even when nothing happens.

'I've never seen anything like it. It was so quiet, I thought it was the end of the world.'

A water pipe breaks under the street and it becomes an earthquake.

Robbie and Miriam sat in the hole. They looked at each other and laughed.

'I've never seen anything like it,' said Robbie.

'It's the biggest small earthquake I've ever seen in my life,' said Miriam.

They fell in love and climbed out of the hole. Two years later, they got married.

'I've never seen anything like it. It was the best wedding ever.'

And a year after that, they had a baby.

Chapter Seven
What Is It about Babies?

People go mad for babies. They just love babies.
Not just human babies – people go mad for all
sorts of babies. They go to the Zoo just to see the
baby elephants and giraffes. It's the wobbly legs
and the tiny trunks. Brainy people become silly
when they see them. Angry people become happy.

'I don't care, I'm going to complain to the
manager – ah, look at the baby parrot's little beak!'

People just love babies. They love talking about
babies and feeding babies and weighing babies
and throwing them in the air and sometimes
catching them and – ah, they just love babies.
Especially yapping about them.

When it comes to babies, the three most used

words in the English language are 'big', 'fat' and 'baby'.

'Will you look at that big fat baby.'

'There's a big fat baby.'

'That's a great big fat baby.'

'That's a grand fat baby.'

'Ah now, look at the size of that baby.'

'That's a good old-fashioned baby. Big and fat.'

Two countries were about to go to war.

'This means war—!'

Until one of the leaders was shown a photograph of a baby.

'Oh, look at the fat on that baby! Is this your baby?'

'Yes,' said the other leader.

'Well, we can forget about the war then. You'll have too much on your hands feeding that baby.'

It wasn't the other leader's baby at all but that doesn't matter. The point is . . . I forget the point. People love babies. Especially when they're big and fat.

But, really, babies aren't big at all. They are tiny.

And this baby was really tiny.

What baby?

The BFB.

The BFB was a tiny little big fat baby. The BFB was a girl, all dressed up in pink, and her granny, Billie Jean Fleetwood-Mack, was carrying her on her back.

Excuse me . . .

Yes?

Why are girl babies always dressed in pink clothes?

I don't know. But later on in the book a seagull called Sam will ask the same question.

Rover and Messi ran to the front gate. Just as
Billie Jean Fleetwood-Mack got there. She'd been
out running with the BFB.

OH NO!

Chapter Eight – Again

Rover and Messi ran to the front gate.

'I'm sick of running to this gate,' said Rover.

'And someone's left it open,' said Messi.

They got there just as Billie Jean Fleetwood-Mack arrived. She'd been out running with the BFB. The BFB was short for the Big Fat Baby. And the Big Fat Baby was Robbie Mack and Miriam Bigge-Mack's little daughter. Her name was Emily. But the family called her the Big Fat Baby, or the BFB.

Billie Jean loved exercise and adventure. She was always climbing mountains or running around the world, for medals and for fun. And these days, she often brought the BFB with her, on her back. She had a special backpack, with a special pocket for carrying a baby. The BFB was in the backpack, and the backpack was up on Billie Jean's back.

She turned at the gate to the house and nearly tripped over Rover.

'Baa!' she shouted.

Really?

No.

'Rover!' Billie Jean shouted.

Rover barked and wagged his tail. Messi barked and thought about all the tangled wires and cables at the back of a television.

'Where are you going?' Billie Jean asked Rover.

She didn't expect an answer. She didn't know that Rover could talk. She didn't know that all dogs can talk. It is one of the best-kept secrets in the history of dogs and people. Kids know that dogs can talk. They talk to the dogs and, now and again, the dogs talk back.

'Goo goo,' says the kid.

'Gaa gaa,' says the dog.

The kids tell their parents about it.

'Doggie can talk!'

'Yes, I know. Eat your carrots.'

'*Can!*'

'I know.'

'*Cannnnnn!*'

But, as they grow up, kids forget that dogs can talk. Sometimes they even forget that other people can talk. But that's a different story.

'Are you going to the shops?' Billie Jean asked Rover.

People love having conversations with dogs. Because the dogs don't answer back.

Rover wagged his tail. Messi thought about crumbs.

'Well,' said Billie Jean. 'We're going inside for lunch. Aren't we, BFB?'

Rover couldn't see the BFB because the BFB was deep inside the backpack.

But he heard her.

'Goop!' she said.

'She must be hungry,' said Billie Jean. 'Are you hungry, BFB?'

'Goop!' said the BFB.

'Off we go, so,' said Billie Jean, and she ran to the front door.

Rover and Messi ran out the gate and – just a few metres away – they saw a perfect example of what they were looking for.

REMINDER: They were looking for dog poo.

'We'd better be careful, Messi,' said Rover, very happily. 'It might bite.'

Rover said this every time they found a good, profitable poo. So Messi didn't really hear him.

But he did hear the scream.

Did the poo scream?

No. But Messi thought it did.

He stared at it.

'The poo just screamed, Uncle Rover,' he said.

'Ah now, Messi,' said Rover. 'It didn't.'

'Yes, it did,' said Messi.

'No, son. It didn't.'

'But I heard it,' said Messi.

'It wasn't me,' said the poo. 'I didn't scream.'

Really?

No. Poos can't talk. Or scream. But people can. And do. And they – Messi, Rover and the poo – heard the scream again.

'Come on, Messi,' said Rover.

He knew the voice. He knew who'd screamed. It was Billie Jean.

Rover ran back through the gate, to the front door of the Mack's house. The door was still open and he saw Billie Jean in the hall. The backpack was no longer on her back. She had taken it off and put it gently on the floor beside her. She was looking into the backpack when Rover arrived.

She looked all around her. Then she looked into the backpack again.

'It's empty,' said Billie Jean.

She looked at Rover.

'Where's the BFB?' she asked.

'Goop!' said something.

Billie Jean and Rover heard it. And so did Messi. But they couldn't see it. They couldn't see the thing that went 'Goop!'

'Goop!' it went again.

They looked around but there wasn't much to look at. They were in the hall. There was the front door and three other doors. There were photographs of various Macks and Fleetwoods and there was a painting of a fig-roll on a horse that Mister Mack had been given when he retired. There was the stairs. There was the rug.

'Goop!'

Billie Jean looked into the backpack again. She picked it up and put her head right into it.

'Goop!'

Rover lifted a corner of the rug with his teeth and Messi looked under it. But there was nothing under there. They had all heard a baby but they couldn't see one.

Rover dropped the rug back on the floor and Messi was just straightening it when they heard it again.

'Goop!'

Twice.

'Goop, goop!'

Messi wagged his tail and fell over – and saw her. He saw the BFB looking down at him.

He remembered not to talk in front of the human, and barked.

Rover looked at Messi and saw that he was still lying on his back and looking up at the ceiling.

Rover looked up.

And barked.

Because the BFB – the Big Fat Baby – was up there, hanging off the lampshade.

Rover barked again. And Billie Jean looked up, and saw the BFB smiling back down at her.

'Goop!'

The BFB let go of the lampshade, and Billie Jean held out the backpack just in time to catch her.

'Goop!'

'You're back,' said Billie Jean.

'Goop!' said the BFB.

'Do you know what must have happened?' Billie Jean said to Rover.

He barked.

'When I was coming in,' said Billie Jean, 'I tripped on the rug and fell forward. And the BFB must have flown out of the backpack and grabbed the lampshade!'

'Woof,' said Rover.

'Goop!' said the BFB.

Messi growled. He was trying to straighten the rug but his Uncle Rover was standing on it.

'Well, Emily,' said Billie Jean.

REMINDER: The Big Fat Baby was called Emily.

'Well, Emily,' said Billie Jean. 'We have had an adventure, haven't we?'

'Hello?'

That was the second shock Billie Jean had had in as many minutes. The baby had just said 'Hello?' – and she sounded very like Billie Jean's husband, Mister Mack.

'Hello?'

But the baby hadn't said 'Hello'. Mister Mack had. He was outside. Billie Jean had phoned him when she couldn't find the BFB, and Mister Mack had come straight home on his bike.

Mister Mack cycled a lot since he'd retired. He had worked in a biscuit factory, tasting the biscuits. He missed the job sometimes, especially the fig-rolls. But he didn't miss the boring cream crackers.

Mister Mack was enjoying his retirement. He went out on his bike every morning.

OH NO!

Chapter Nine Is a Bit Annoyed about Being Interrupted by a Cream Cracker, so We'll Move Straight on to –

Chapter Ten

'Hello?' said Mister Mack.

Mister Mack was parking his bike. But he'd
forgotten to get off it first, and he was stuck.
And worried. He still thought the BFB, his lovely
granddaughter, was missing.

'Hello?' he called again.

'Hello,' said Billie Jean.

'Goop!' said the BFB.

It was the nicest sound Mister Mack had ever
heard.

'You found her,' he said.

'Yes,' said Billie Jean.

'What happened?' said Mister Mack.

'Well,' said Billie Jean. 'I've never seen

anything like it. What happened was this . . .'

Rover and Messi had seen what had happened, so they didn't hang around for the story. They were dogs on a mission. The Gigglers were waiting and Rover had to deliver some top-notch Giggler Treatment-ready poo. While Billie Jean started to tell her husband all about the Mystery of the Disappearing Baby, Rover and Messi ran out the gate, to the street and the poo.

They could still hear Billie Jean.

'Well,' said Billie Jean. 'I've never seen anything like it. What happened was this . . .'

'Why does she keep saying the same thing, Uncle Rover?' Messi asked.

'Ignore it,' said Rover. 'It's just that kind of book.'

'Well,' said Billie Jean. 'I've never seen anything like it. What happened was this . . .'

'Ignore it,' said Rover. 'The writer's just trying to annoy us.'

'Well,' said Billie Jean. 'I've never seen anything like it. What happened was this . . .'

'She's still doing it, Uncle Rover,' said Messi.

'It's not the way stories should be told.'

'Well,' said Billie Jean. 'What happened was this – I was out for a run.'

'About time,' said Rover.

'And when I came back,' said Billie Jean, 'I opened the front door and – you know the rug?'

'Yes,' said Mister Mack. 'The rug in the hall?'

'Yes,' said Billie Jean. 'My mother gave it to us when we got married, remember?'

'How is she, by the way?' asked Mister Mack.

Adults are like that. They are always wrecking perfectly good stories. Billie Jean and Mister Mack were going to talk about the rug and Billie Jean's mother for another ten minutes. So if you want to go off and play or read another book or annoy your brother, and come back in, say, nine and a bit minutes, that's fine. Or –

Hey, pal.

Yes, Rover?

Do you think myself and my nephew here are going to hang around all day while you mess around?

You tell him, Uncle Rover.

Time is money. And books shouldn't be messy.

'Alright, Rover,' said the writer. 'I'll cut out the bits about Billie Jean's mother.'

You do that, pal.

'Well,' said Billie Jean. 'I tripped on the rug. And I went head first. Like this.'

She showed Mister Mack how she'd tripped on the rug and shot forward. And, as she did that, the BFB flew out of the backpack – again! – and right over the garden hedge.

'Goop!' said the BFB.

Chapter Eleven
Back to the Gigglers

A small Giggler ran into Giggler Headquarters.
She was even smaller than the smallest Giggler.
She was actually the smallest Giggler never seen.
She was tiny – really, really tiny. But she had a big
voice.

'POO!'

'Where?!' said the biggest Giggler.

'WE NEED MORE POO!' the tiny, tiny Giggler
explained.

'Why?'

'GROWN-UP JUST CALLED LITTLE BOY A
FEATHER-HEAD!'

'Why?'

'NO REASON!'

'Sure?'

'NO REASON AT ALL!'

'Right,' said Biggest.

'SAID IT THREE TIMES!'

'Right, so,' said Biggest. 'We can't be having that. The Giggler Treatment for him. We'll need more poo.'

'GROWN-UP HAS BIG FEET!'

'Lots more poo,' said the biggest Giggler. 'Any sign of Rover?'

Chapter Twelve

Rover was just about to pick up the poo when the BFB flew over his head. Her shadow shot across the footpath.

'Either that was a very fast cloud, or a big fat baby just flew over our heads,' Rover said to Messi.

'The postman's bike is mucky,' said Messi.

The postman was actually a woman. Her name was Etna Stamp and she was cycling past just as the BFB sailed over Rover and Messi.

Etna had had a rough day, so far. It had rained on her five times – so far – and a bulldog called Sweetie had tried to bite the back wheel off her bike. She'd had ten extra parcels to deliver to a woman who lived at the top of the steepest hill in Dublin. Her feet felt heavy and sore as she pushed the pedals of her bike.

The thing Etna liked most about her job was reading all the letters before she delivered them. She wasn't being nosey and she never told anybody else what was in the letters.

If there was bad news in a letter, Etna would ring the doorbell, so she could chat to whoever was going to read the bad news. She would tell them that they were looking great or that their new jumper was lovely. To make them feel a little bit more cheerful before they read the bad news. Etna thought that this was the most important part of her job.

But she hadn't been able to read the letters this morning. Because the post office kettle had been broken.

It was like this.

I know.

Who's that?

The reader.

And what do you know?

How the post lady read the letters. She held the
envelopes over the steam coming out of the kettle
until, like, she was able to open the envelope without
ripping it. Then she took the letter out and read it,
like. Then she put it back in the envelope and closed it
again. And, like, she waved the envelope around a bit,
to dry it.

How did you know that?

I open my parents' letters all the time.

OK.

Especially the reports from school, like.

OK.

And any letter that looks like it might have money
in it.

OK. Anyway, Etna wasn't happy. She was
a nice woman but it hadn't been a nice day.
She was cycling on a flat piece of the road but,
suddenly, it felt as if the bike was getting heavier.
She had delivered all the post, so cycling back to
the post office should have been easy.

But it wasn't.

Etna's legs were sore.

'I'm getting old,' she told herself, as she pushed

her feet down on the pedals.

But Etna wasn't getting old.

Well, she was. She was thirty seconds older than she had been when she'd cycled past Rover and Messi. But her bike didn't feel heavier because she was getting older. Etna's bike seemed heavier – Etna's bike *was* heavier – because the BFB had landed on it. The BFB had dropped into the leather pouch where Etna carried her letters and parcels. Etna was cycling away with the BFB.

'Goop!' said the BFB.

But Etna didn't hear her. Because Etna was a bit deaf.

What?

Etna was a bit deaf.

Chapter Thirteen

When Billie Jean and Mister Mack got out to where Rover and Messi were standing on the kerb, there was no sign of the BFB.

'Maybe she hasn't landed yet,' said Mister Mack.

He looked up at the sky.

Rover barked. He understood humans. They were a bit slow sometimes, especially parents and grandparents. After years of looking after children their brains turned to mush.

Rover barked again. Messi joined in – because he liked barking.

'What is it, Rover?' Billie Jean asked.

Rover couldn't point at Etna Stamp cycling

away. He wanted to, but he couldn't. Dogs can't lift their front legs and point.

Rover could talk but he wasn't going to. It is, of course, one of the world's best-kept secrets: animals can talk – especially dogs. But it isn't the only one.

OTHER WELL-KEPT SECRETS

Many people go to school and end up thinking that science teachers are aliens. But they're not. Science teachers are actually experiments performed by other, older science teachers. Now, if your teacher is brainy enough to invent another teacher, then he or she is well worth listening to. So the fact that your science teacher is an artificial life form who stays behind after work to make other artificial life forms is very good news.

Another one of the world's best-kept secrets is this: vegetables are evil, especially the green ones. And the idea that eating vegetables is good for you is a big fat green lie that was started by vegetables, helped by vegetarians. Vegetarians are people who pretend to like eating vegetables but secretly eat burgers and chicken nuggets in the same room where the science teachers are inventing other science teachers. The only honest vegetables are beans. But they aren't really vegetables at all. They are legumes.

They are Lego?

No – legumes. Beans are legumes.

What's a legume?

I'm not sure but it's not a vegetable, although it's nearly a vegetable – kind of. The beans try to warn the humans that vegetables are evil and that they are trying to take over the world. The beans shout it.

'Watch out, people! The vegetables are evil!'

But no one can hear them because they are in tins. And when they escape, they are so stunned – the sunshine, the fresh air, the chips! – that they forget they have an important message to shout. And by the time they remember, they have been eaten.

And that's another secret. Farts are actually the beans in your tummy shouting,

Back to the story – for a while.

The Return of
Chapter Thirteen

Rover barked again.

He looked, and saw that Billie Jean and Mister Mack were looking at him.

Then he ran.

He ran as fast as he could after Etna and her bike. He knew they'd watch him and they'd see him catching up on Etna. And he hoped they would think, 'Aha! The BFB is in Etna's pouch!'

One thing helped.

The BFB popped her head out of the pouch.

'Goop!' she said.

One thing didn't help.

Rover wasn't as young as he used to be. He could still run, but not as fast or for as long. He

could run, but Rover had always thought that
running was a bit stupid.

All dogs are like this. They chase the balls their
owners throw for them but, really, they would
much prefer it if the owners ran after their own
sticks and balls and plastic toys. And that is often
what happens. People run after the sticks they
throw for their dogs and the dogs stay behind and
watch them.

Anyway.

One more thing helped.

Messi had run after his Uncle Rover. In fact,
Messi had gone past Rover – although he didn't
know yet what they were running after. But he
was a pup, and fast and full of beans – *Watch out,
people!* – and he wanted to run as fast as he could.
He hadn't learned yet that running was stupid.
So he shot past Rover. And that made Rover run
faster. He wasn't going to let his little nephew win
this race. And he went past Messi.

'Keep in touch, Messi,' he said.

He was now very close to Etna and her bike.

Messi ran past Rover again and Rover went

even faster to catch up with him.

'Why are we running, Uncle Rover?' he asked.

One more thing didn't help.

Rover had no breath left to tell Messi why they were running and Messi ran straight past Etna Stamp and her baby-filled bicycle.

One wet thing helped.

There was a ramp – a speed bump – right across the street, in front of Etna. It was brand new. In fact, it was still wet. Etna cycled on to it. She cycled *into* it. Etna cycled straight into the wet cement, and stopped. The front wheel was stuck.

But this was bad too. Because the rest of the bike was lifted into the air and the BFB flew out of the letters pouch—

Again?

Again.

And up into the air.

Chapter Fourteen

Billie Jean had started to run after Rover, and Mister Mack had gone back into the garden to get his bike.

Billie Jean texted as she ran. She texted her son, Robbie. Robbie was the BFB's dad. *BFB has escaped again. X.* She also sent the text to her other son, Jimmy, and her daughter, Kayla. She even sent it to Mister Mack, just in case he forgot. He was in the front garden with his bike, trying to remember why he'd gone back in, when he heard the text and read it.

'Oh, yes,' he said, and hopped on the bike.

Back to the BFB.

She had flown up into the air – and down – into a handbag.

The back wheel of Etna's bike landed back on the road. Luckily the bike hadn't flipped over, so Etna was fine. She got off the bike and looked at the front wheel. She let go of the handlebars and the bike didn't fall over.

Rover had caught up with Etna, and Billie Jean had caught up with Rover.

Billie Jean looked into Etna's pouch.

Was Etna a kangaroo?

No! She wasn't even nearly a kangaroo.

OH NO!

Chapter Fourteen
Back by Popular Demand!

Billie Jean looked into the pouch but the BFB wasn't in there.

'Did you post Emily, Etna?' she asked.

'Did she have a stamp on her?' Etna asked.

'No, she didn't,' said Billie Jean.

'Well, then I didn't,' said Etna.

She pulled the front wheel out of the wet cement. It had been a long day. Etna just wanted to go home.

Rover barked.

Meanwhile, the owner of the handbag was getting on to the number 39A bus.

This time nobody had seen the BFB flying through the air. Not Rover, not Billie Jean, not

Mister Mack, not the owner of the handbag.

And definitely not Messi.

He was still charging down the street like a mad thing.

Rover barked again.

Messi kept going.

This time, Rover had to shout.

'Messi!'

Messi heard him.

But no one else did.

Well, they did. But they were too busy and much too worried to notice. They were looking for the BFB.

Messi stopped and turned and saw his Uncle Rover. And he ran straight across the street, right in front of a white van.

The white van screeched to a stop.

The driver's window was open.

'Watch where you're going, pup!' the driver shouted.

Then he started the white van again and continued on his journey to the airport.

Messi kept running, until he got back to Rover.

Rover hid behind a bin, so the humans wouldn't hear him giving out to Messi.

'You nearly got smacked by that white van there, Messi.'

'I'd have smacked it back, Uncle Rover,' said Messi.

He was a tough little dog.

'Listen, Messi,' said Rover. 'If that van had hit you there'd be blood and guts everywhere. Think of the mess.'

'Sorry, Uncle Rover,' said Messi.

Meanwhile, Billie Jean and Mister Mack were still standing at the wet speed bump.

'What will we do?' asked Mister Mack.

Robbie Mack arrived. He jumped out of his car.

'Where is she?' he asked.

'She's around here somewhere,' said Billie Jean.

'We'll have to search everywhere between here and the house,' said Robbie.

Rover put his mouth to Messi's ear.

'I know where she is,' he whispered.

Messi fell over.

'Where?' he asked when he stood up.

'The white van,' said Rover. 'The windows were all open. She must have gone in through the window.'

He barked.

But the humans didn't notice. They were looking in the shop windows. This wasn't the first time that the BFB had gone on an adventure. They had once found her in the wine-shop window, sitting in among the bottles of wine.

Rover barked again.

But the humans still didn't notice.

So Rover shouted. 'The van!'

'What van?' Mister Mack asked.

He was looking in the bakery window.

'The white van!' Rover shouted.

'I saw a white van when I was parking,' said Robbie. 'Quick!'

'Where?' said Mister Mack, and he ran to his bike.

'Quick,' said Robbie. 'That was the word on the side of the white van.'

'Only one word?'

'Quick Couriers,' said Robbie. 'Anywhere In the World, We'll Get It There Pronto.'

'Oh, no!' said Billie Jean. 'That means the BFB could be going anywhere in the world.'

'And pronto.'

'Let's go,' said Robbie.

He ran to his car.

'Oh, no!'

Robbie had parked his car on the wet speed bump. But it wasn't wet any more. The cement was dry and the front wheels of the car were stuck in it.

Robbie grabbed his father's bike.

'Sorry, Dad,' he said. 'This is an emergency.'

'We'll stay here,' said Billie Jean. 'We'll search all the gardens and shop windows.'

'OK,' said Robbie, and he took off on the bike.

The white van was a distant white dot.

Rover and Messi ran after Robbie.

'What about the Gigglers, Uncle Rover?' Messi asked.

'What about them?'

'They're waiting for their poo,' said Messi.

'They'll have to wait,' said Rover. 'We have to catch up with the BFB. And ASAP.'

What does ASAP mean?

Sorry, we're in a hurry.

Chapter Fifteen
A Very Short Little Chapter

Meanwhile, the BFB had found lots of interesting stuff in the handbag. It wasn't the first time she'd been in that bag.

Chapter Sixteen

The Gigglers had been waiting. And waiting and waiting. For Rover. They had ordered seventeen dog poos, to give thirteen adults – seven men and six women – the Giggler Treatment.

That's only thirteen.

What?

7 + 6 = 13. You said the Gigglers were waiting for seventeen poos but they were only going to give the Giggler Treatment to thirteen adults.

But one of the adults was a total eejit and Gigglers knew they'd have to give him the Treatment four times before he learned the lesson. 7 + 6 + 4 (Eejit) = 17.

Anyway, the Gigglers were hiding behind their

favourite wall. A cranky mam was on her way. She always took this route when she was on her way to her angry-yoga class. The Gigglers were going to give her the Treatment because she had made her twin daughters count all the crispies in a large box of cereal.

'So I can have a bit of peace and quiet, if that's not too much to ask for,' she'd said. 'I have a life too, you know.'

She'd gone really mad when she saw that the girls had drawn little faces on every crispie. There were hundreds of little smiling faces looking up at her when she picked up the box and looked in.

'You're driving me mad, girls,' she'd said. 'This is *so* not OK.'

The girls had to wipe the faces off each crispie.

'And make sure they're still crispy,' said their mam. 'I'll be checking every one of them.'

The twins had to dry each crispie with a hairdryer. One twin held the dryer and the other held the crispie so it wouldn't blow away. It was nearly midnight by the time they'd finished and gone to bed. They were falling asleep at the same

time. They closed
their eyes at the
exact same
moment.

'What do
you see?' a
twin asked her
sister.

'Crispies,'
said the twin's
twin sister.
'Like, millions of crispies.'

'Me too,' said the twin. 'Millions and millions of
crispies.'

'Do yours have faces?'

'Little evil faces.'

'Like, millions and millions of little evil faces.'

The twins didn't sleep a wink because all of the
crispies snored.

'Snoring crispies, like.'

'Millions and millions of little evil snoring
crispies.'

The Gigglers had seen and heard all of this

because the tiny, tiny Giggler had been hiding in the cornflakes box right beside the crispies.

So the Gigglers were now behind their wall, waiting for the twins' mam. They knew she'd be wearing her brand-new green gym shoes. They knew that one of those shoes was going to plonk itself down on a good old-fashioned dollop of dog poo.

But they didn't have the poo. Those gym shoes were going to go straight past the Gigglers, still green and very clean.

'Where is Rover?' the biggest Giggler whispered.

'DON'T KNOW!' said the tiny, tiny Giggler.

'Shhhhh!'

'SORRY!'

'I texted him,' said the smaller Giggler. 'But he hasn't answered.'

Chapter Seventeen

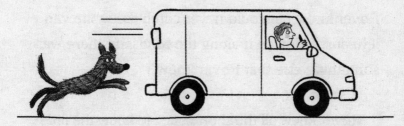

Where *was* Rover?

He was running after the white van and he was well on his way to the airport.

He knew the Gigglers were waiting for him and he knew he was letting them down. But he knew they would understand when they found out why he wasn't doing what he was supposed to be doing – bringing them poo. He really wanted to catch up with the white van, so he could get back to work. But vans with engines are quick, and middle-aged dogs with big bellies—

WHAT?

Sorry, Rover. Even elderly dogs—

WHAT?!

Even middle-aged dogs who exercise regularly and are very careful about what they eat – these dogs start off fast but they have to slow down. Rover knew he would never catch the white van if he just followed it along the road. But there was something else that Rover knew.

A short cut.

Rover knew all the short cuts. He knew the little lanes and secret corners that no one else knew. He knew about tunnels that went under whole cities and countries. He knew that jumping over a wall often made much more sense than going around it.

Robbie on his dad's bike was way ahead of Rover. But Rover knew a short cut.

OH NO!

85

Chapter Seventeen . . .
Isn't Over Yet

While the evil crispies were taking over the world, Rover was remembering the best short cut to the airport.

'Messi,' he said.

'Yes, Uncle Rover?' said Messi.

He was running right beside his uncle.

'We're taking a short cut,' said Rover.

'Hmmmmm,' said Messi.

Messi didn't like short cuts. They were kind of messy and often dirty and sometimes they just looked like mistakes. Roads that hadn't been finished, holes in walls that hadn't been built properly, mucky tracks across lovely green grass.

'Yeah,' said Rover. 'We're going to crawl under this hedge here and then run across a couple of fields.'

'Hmmmmmmm,' said Messi.

'And I don't want to hear any objections,' said Rover. 'We have to catch that baby. OK?'

'OK,' said Messi.

He followed his uncle under the hedge.

'Do we have time to trim it, Uncle Rover?'

'Not this time, Messi, no,' said Rover.

'There's a plastic bag in the hedge, Uncle Rover,' said Messi. 'Will I bring it?'

'Why?'

'To pick up the poo.'

'What poo?' Rover asked.

'The poo you're standing in, Uncle Rover.'

Rover looked down. He had climbed out from under the hedge and he was standing in a field near some cows. In fact, he was standing in the middle of a big cow-poo pancake.

'Brilliant,' said Rover.

He meant it.

'So, Messi,' he said. 'What's the plan?'

'We collect the poo while we go after the baby,' said Messi.

Messi had been on rescue missions with Rover before. They always ended up charging around the world. Messi was a well-travelled little dog.

'International poos of the world,' said Messi.

Rover said it again. 'Brilliant.'

'And we'll start with this Irish cow poo,' said Messi. 'After you step out of it, that is.'

'You're a bit of a genius, Messi,' said Rover.

'I don't like bits,' said Messi.

'You're a whole genius then,' said Rover.

Messi could feel his tail going fizzy.

'Nappies!' he shouted.

Chapter Eighteen

Meanwhile – it's that word again:

Meanwhile, Billie Jean and Mister Mack were searching in all the gardens – up trees, under bushes, on top of bird tables – for the BFB.

Meanwhile, Robbie was cycling after the white van, and the white van had nearly reached the airport.

Meanwhile, the BFB's mother, Miriam Bigge-Mack, was also cycling to the airport. So was Robbie's brother, Jimmy.

Meanwhile, a hand went into the handbag. The owner of the bag was sitting upstairs on the 39A bus. She put her hand into her bag to take out her phone. But, instead, she took out . . .

'Emily!'

'Goop!' said the BFB.

REMINDER: The BFB is still called Emily.

'What are you doing in my bag?' asked Kayla Mack.

'Goop,' said the BFB.

'You weren't in there earlier,' said Kayla.

'Goop,' the BFB agreed.

'How's life?'

'Goop.'

'Cool,' said Kayla. 'Here, sit up on my lap and you can look out the window.'

Kayla was eighteen but she remembered when she was a baby. The two things she'd liked most as a child were looking out of bus windows and jumping out of windows – but never jumping out of bus windows.

So Kayla cuddled the BFB as they both looked out the window at all the houses and people and

white vans. Kayla was the BFB's dad's sister. So
that made her the BFB's aunt. She liked being an
aunt and the BFB was her favourite niece. She
was also her only niece.

'Where's your dad?' she asked.

'Goop.'

'Where's your mam?'

'Goop.'

'Where's Granny Billie Jean?'

'Goop.'

'And Granddad?'

'Goop,' said the BFB.

Kayla was searching for her phone in her bag.

The last time she'd seen the BFB, she'd been
in the kitchen with Kayla's mother, Billie Jean.
So she was going to phone Billie Jean, to tell her
that the BFB had crawled into her bag. Kayla
knew that her mother would be searching for the
missing baby. She'd be worried and wondering
where she was. Kayla would phone her now and
tell her.

But she couldn't find the phone.

It wasn't in her bag.

Kayla liked her phone but she didn't like it that much. She didn't carry it everywhere. When she wanted to know what the weather was like, she didn't google 'Dublin weather'. She looked out the window and saw the rain. She often forgot her phone – sometimes on purpose. You could be really sarcastic when you didn't have a phone.

'Oh my God! Do you not, like, have a phone?'

'Oh my God, yeah. But it's, like, invisible.'

The Last Bit of
Chapter Eighteen

So, Kayla wasn't able to phone Billie Jean because she'd left her phone on top of her bed at home.

Now she had a nice idea.

'Do you want to come to college with me?' she asked the BFB.

'Goop,' said the BFB.

'Cool,' said Kayla. 'Let's count the red cars.'

'Goop?'

'No, the red ones.'

Kayla would phone Billie Jean when she got off the bus at the college.

Kayla had just started college. She loved it. She was studying maths and sarcasm at BBFOSID – Big Building Full Of Students In Dublin.

Chapter Nineteen

Sometimes short cuts just aren't enough. Rover and Messi made it to the airport at the same time that Robbie and Miriam got there.

They found a car park full of white vans.

Empty white vans.

Hundreds of them.

But then they saw one parked near a white plane. A white plane which was starting to move.

'Oh, no!'

It moved slowly down the runway.

'Oh, no!'

Then faster.

'Woof!'

And faster.

'Oh, no!'

They watched the plane climb slowly up and up, into the air.

'Oh, no, no, no, no!'

They cycled and ran across to the white van.

'Excuse me,' said Miriam. 'Was there a baby in your van?'

'What?' said the driver. 'Are you mad? I'd never bring the baby to work.'

'What baby?'

'My baby,' said the driver.

'But was there a baby in the van when you were loading the things on to the plane?'

'No,' said the driver.

'Are you sure?' Robbie asked him.

'. . . No,' said the driver.

'Where's the plane going?'

'Casablanca,' said the driver.

'Where's that?' Miriam asked.

Messi knew the answer.

'Morocco,' said the driver.

Messi fell over.

IMPORTANT INFORMATION

Remember: this was not the first time the BFB had gone off on an adventure. Here are some of the places she'd gone to before:

the back garden;
the front garden;
the wine-shop window;
the butcher's window;
on top of the ice-cream machine in the Spar;
Galway;
the press under the sink in the kitchen;
the little room under the stairs;
Sweden;
the attic;
the next-door
    neighbour's shed;
under Kayla's bed;
Japan.

Chapter Twenty

It took Kayla a while to learn how to use the phone. It was on a wall and you had to put money into it. Eventually, with the BFB's help – 'Goop!' – she was able to use it.

But then she couldn't remember Granny Billie Jean's number.

But the BFB did.

'Goop goop goop, goop, goop goop, goop goop goop goop.'

'Cool,' said Kayla. 'Thanks.'

The phone rang and rang.

'Why doesn't she answer?'

Then Kayla heard her mother's message.

Hi – I'm not able to answer right now . . .

Obviously – ha ha ha ha.

'That's, like, so embarrassing,' said Kayla.

The BFB didn't agree.

'Goop,' she said.

Just leave a message and I'll get back to you. Promise!

'Hi,' said Kayla. 'It's me – your daughter. Emily is with me. She crawled into my bag. Again. Anyway, she's fine. Say hi, Emily.'

'Goop!'

'See you later,' said Kayla. 'We're going to a class now. Bye – I suppose.'

She put the thing you speak into on top of the other thing.

'They're kind of cool, aren't they?' she said. 'Old phones, like?'

'Goop!' the BFB agreed.

'Right,' said Kayla. 'Sarcasm for Beginners. Does that sound good, Emily?'

'Goop!'

Chapter Twenty-One
Robbie Remembers

Kids know lots of things. But adults think kids are stupid.

Excuse me – we do not.

Who's that?

I'm an adult.

OK.

A very important adult, actually.

OK. This is how it is. Adults love their kids. They think kids are sweet, lovely, charming, brainy, funny and wonderful. Am I right?

Well, mine are.

But they also think that kids know nothing. That kids are small and their heads are small, so there's no room for important things in those small heads. That is what adults think. But this is a big, big mistake. Because kids know a lot. In fact, kids know all the things that are worth knowing.

Here are just some of the things that kids know:

eating fish is stupid;
holes in the ground are interesting;
worms are cool;
mice are cool and not cool at the exact
    same time;
shoelaces are stupid;
dogs can talk.

But, as they grow up and get older, kids forget most of these things. They eat fish. They walk straight past holes without looking in them. And they never, ever think that the voice speaking behind them might belong to a dog.

But Robbie remembered.

'Rover,' he said.

Rover barked.

'Listen, Rover,' said Robbie. 'I know you can talk.'

Rover barked.

'I remember it, Rover,' said Robbie.

He leaned down and patted Rover's head.

'Who's a good dog?' he asked.

'Me,' said Rover.

'You admit that you can talk?' said Robbie.

'OK,' said Rover. 'Yeah.'

'Me too,' said Messi.

Robbie patted Messi.

'Tea-bags in the sink!' Messi shouted, and he didn't fall over.

'We have to catch up with that plane,' said Robbie. 'We need a short cut to Morocco.'

'No problem,' said Rover. 'Follow me.'

'And me,' said Messi.

Rover and Messi ran across the airport runway, to a big patch of grass.

Anybody who has ever looked out of a plane window while it's on the runway will know that rabbits love airports. Look out of a plane window and you will see a rabbit sitting in the grass looking back at you. You will probably see more rabbits than you've ever seen before. The rabbits

don't really
live *in* the
airport. They
live *under* the
airport. Under
every airport
there are
burrows
and tunnels that are as big as cities.

And this is the brilliant bit. There are so many
airports all over the world, so close to each
other, that all of the rabbit burrows and tunnels
have joined up to become one huge rabbit city.
It is actually quicker to go from Dublin to Paris
through the rabbit burrows than it is to fly. But
only the rabbits know this.

And one Irish dog.

Hmmmmmmm.

Two Irish dogs.

The Dublin Airport rabbits saw Rover running
at them. Rabbits usually don't like dogs, but they
liked Rover. Because he paid them to use their
tunnels. So they didn't run or hide. They just

stood out of the way and let Rover go past them.

'How's it going, lads?' Rover asked as he ran past the rabbits.

'Groovy,' said one of the rabbits.

Rabbits can talk but they only use three words. One of them is 'groovy' and other two are 'not so'.

'It might rain later,' said Rover.

'Not so groovy,' said the rabbit.

There was a small bush in front of Rover. Three rabbits pulled back the bush and there, right in front of Rover, was a huge hole. He ran straight into it, followed by Messi, followed by Miriam on her bike, followed by Robbie on his dad's bike,

and followed by his brother, Jimmy, who had just arrived, on his bike.

A little boy was sitting in the window seat, looking out of the window, waiting for his plane to take off.

'Daddy,' he said. 'Two doggies and two mans and a lady and *twee* bi-clickles just fell down a hole.'

'Yes, Cormac.'

'Did.'

'I know.'

By the time the boy's dad looked out of the window, the rabbits had dropped the bush back on top of the hole. Rover and the rest were well on their way to Casablanca.

Excuse me . . .

Yes?

They're going to Casablanca to find the BFB?

Yes, they are.

But she isn't there. She's with Kayla. So it's a waste of time, isn't it?

No. It isn't. It seems like it is, but it isn't. Their timing will have to be perfect.

Chapter Twenty-Two
Education

While Rover and the others ran underground to Morocco, Kayla sat in a classroom with the BFB on her knee.

'Oh,' said one of the other students. 'Is that your baby?'

'No,' said Kayla. 'It's my granny.'

'That was excellent work, Kayla,' said the sarcasm teacher. 'A top-class smart answer. I hope you were all listening.'

The teacher's name was Dr Holly Notte-Lykely. She was one of the world's greatest experts on smart answers.

'Now, Kayla,' said Dr Notte-Lykely. 'Will you, please, pass the baby on to the next student.'

The next student was a young man called Kevin. Kayla put the BFB on his knee. The BFB looked very happy there. She looked up at Kevin, pulled his beard and laughed.

'Now,' said Dr Notte-Lykely. 'Somebody ask Kevin the question.'

'Oh, Kevin,' said Kayla. 'Is that your baby?'

'Eh – no,' said Kevin.

'That wasn't very sarcastic,' said Dr Notte-Lykely.

'Goop,' the BFB agreed.

'Eh,' said Kevin. 'I think I'm after making a mistake. I don't think I should be here. I thought, like, sarcasm was about rock climbing.'

'Really?'

'Yeah, maybe,' said Kevin, very sarcastically. 'As if.'

He had fooled all of the others in the room.

'Excellent,' said Dr Notte-Lykely. 'Let's hear a big clap for Kevin – not! Pass the baby.'

'Goop,' said the BFB.

She was having a great time.

Chapter Twenty-Three

The Gigglers were still hiding behind the wall. But now they were waiting for a different grown-up. They were going to give the Treatment to a swimming teacher who kept telling a little boy that he swam like a bag of cement.

The swimming teacher was the total eejit who would have to get the Treatment four times before he learned his lesson.

The Gigglers could hear him coming. He was wearing wet flip-flops. So they could hear his big feet going *slap*, *slap*, *slap* on the path. They really wanted to hear one of those big flippy-floppy feet smacking the poo.

But they had no poo and there was no sign of Rover.

'We might have to look for another dog,' said the biggest Giggler.

Chapter Twenty-Four
Every Short Cut Leads to Poo

Rover, Messi, Jimmy, Miriam and Robbie
ran and cycled under a lot of Europe and the
Mediterranean Sea.

It was dark all the way.

Except when they met a rabbit with a torch.

'*Merci*, pal,' said Rover when they passed the
rabbit under Paris.

'*Mais* groooovy!' said the French rabbit, shining
the torch for them.

Miriam, Robbie and Jimmy could feel the roofs
of the tunnels right over their heads. Sometimes
they could feel their hair rubbing the mucky
ceiling. And they could feel the stones and roots
under the wheels of their bikes. They knew that

they might cycle into something big, and fall. But they didn't slow down. They had to find the BFB.

Rover was tired.

He didn't run a lot these days. But today – so far – he had run under the Irish Sea, England, the English Channel, France, Spain and the Mediterranean Sea.

And it was still the morning.

'Look!'

There was the tunnel and there was light. And the light was where Rover wanted it, at the end of the tunnel.

'Nearly there,' said Rover.

He took a deep, deep breath – and ran.

The light got bigger and rounder.

'Nearly . . . there . . .'

The light got a little bit bigger.

'. . . nearly . . . . there.'

And bigger.

Then it seemed to get a bit smaller.

No, it didn't.

It got bigger – until they could see that the roof above them was higher. The tunnel was wider too, and they could all see properly now, because the sunlight was coming in.

They charged out, into the middle of the Sahara Desert.

'And here we are,' said Rover.

'Wow,' said the three humans.

'Oh,' said Messi. 'Oh.'

He stood looking at the sand.

All of the sand.

All over the place.

'It's beautiful,' said Miriam.

'It's messy,' said Messi.

'Calm down, Messi,' said Rover.

'We have to tidy it up, Uncle Rover,' said Messi.

'Not today, Messi.'

'Hmmmmmm,' said Messi.

'We don't have time,' said Rover. 'Besides, it's a desert.'

'It's too sandy,' said Messi.

'It's supposed to be sandy,' said Rover.

'Hmmmmmmmmm,' said Messi.

'There's the airport!' said Miriam.

She pointed at it, across the sand.

'Come on!'

They started cycling over the sand. But it wasn't easy. It was hard work. The muscles in their legs weren't very happy.

But they kept going.

Messi cheered up when he saw a camel.

'Camel poo, Uncle Rover,' he said.

'Good man, Messi,' said Rover.

While the others charged towards Casablanca Airport, Messi ran up to the camel and scooped his poo into the bag with the cow poo.

'Thanks,' he said.

'Groovy,' said the camel, who thought he was a rabbit.

Messi ran nearly as fast as he could and caught up with the others.

Just in time to see a white plane taking off.

'Oh, no!'

'Where's that plane going, pal?' Rover asked a Moroccan rabbit.

The rabbit pointed east.

They all tried to think of places east of Casablanca.

'Algiers?' said Jimmy.

The rabbit shook his head.

'Tunis?' said Miriam.

The rabbit shook his head.

'Tripoli?' said Robbie.

And the rabbit shook his head.

'It must be Cairo then,' said Rover.

But the rabbit shook his head.

Messi knew his geography.

'Tel Aviv?' he said.

The rabbit gave his head a shake.

'Beirut?'

The rabbit shook his head.

'Come on, come on,' said Robbie. 'We have

to find Emily. Istanbul?'

'Groovy,' said the rabbit, and he nodded
his head.

Chapter Twenty-Six

Kayla and the BFB had been in BBFOSID for two whole hours.

'Will we go home now, Emily?' said Kayla.

'Like, goop,' said the BFB.

She liked being a student but she wanted to go home to her mammy and her dad and her granny and her granddad and the fridge.

'Right,' said Kayla. 'We'll go home. Bus or choo-choo?'

'Goop-goop.'

'Good choice,' said Kayla.

She put the BFB into her bag. But she made sure the BFB had a good view. Her little head was sticking straight out of the bag, looking at the world go by.

'Ah, look at the baby in the bag.'

'Like, goop,' said the BFB.

Chapter Twenty-Seven
Is Sponsored by Bunny Tunnels

Are you afraid of flying? Let **Bunny Tunnels** get you there!

Rover, Messi and the others cycled and ran all the way under North Africa. Somewhere under Egypt, Rover asked Jimmy for a lift.

'Getting a bit old for running, Rover?' said Jimmy.

'Yeah, yeah – whatever,' said Rover.

He climbed up Jimmy's leg and decided not to bite it. He sat on the crossbar of Jimmy's bike. Jimmy had to cycle extra hard now because Rover was the only one who knew the way to Istanbul, so he had to stay at the front.

They came to a place where the tunnel divided into two tunnels.

'Stay to the left,' said Rover.

Soon they could see the light.

The light got bigger and brighter.

'Istanbul here we come!'

They came to the end of the tunnel and ran and cycled out – and saw Rome.

'Sorry, lads,' said Rover. 'I'm always mixing up my lefts and my rights.'

They turned and charged back in. This time they went down the other tunnel and five minutes later they came out, blinking, at Istanbul Airport – just in time to see a white plane taking off.

'Oh, no!'

There was a rabbit sitting in the dry grass beside the runway.

'Where's that plane going, pal?' Rover asked her.

The rabbit pointed west.

'Sofia?' said Robbie.

The rabbit shook her head.

'Belgrade?' said Miriam.

The rabbit shook her head.

'Vienna?' said Jimmy.

The rabbit shook her head.

'Düsseldorf?' said Messi.

And the rabbit shook her head.

'OK,' said Rover. 'Amsterdam?'

But the rabbit shook her head.

'London?'

The rabbit gave her head a shake.

'What?' said Rover. 'Dublin?'

'Groovy,' said the rabbit.

'All the way back to where we started!'

'Come on!' said Robbie, and he put his foot down on the pedal.

Messi was busy collecting poo. Some goat

poo, sheep poo, wildcat poo, long-eared bat poo, handy rabbit poo and European mole poo went into the bag, beside the camel poo and the good old Irish cow poo.

The bag was heavy and on his back. But Messi was very happy with his poo collection. He could feel his tail starting to wag and he knew he had to stop it. If he didn't, he'd fall over and he wouldn't be able to get up quickly again because the bag was so heavy.

But there was a problem.

He was running out of messy things to shout. He had gone through all the socks and towels and tea-bags and dirty dishes. But his tail was getting waggier and he'd have to shout something very soon or he'd fall over.

He thought of something.

'Deserts!' he shouted.

It worked. His tail slowed down but it didn't stop.

Little messes seemed to work better.

He thought of another big one.

'Volcanoes!'

This time his tail stopped wagging. Now he could run to Dublin.

He turned, just in time to see the back wheel of the last bike going back down the rabbit hole.

He ran after it.

A Very Short Chapter That Doesn't Even Seem to Be Part of the Book But Is

Paddy O'Leary was hungry.

'I think I'll have some beans on toast,' he said.

Chapter Twenty-Eight
Is Probably the Last Chapter

Kayla and the BFB were sitting on the train. They were looking out at all the back gardens and garages and walls and sheds and lanes and volcanoes.

The train was slowing down.

'Our stop next,' Kayla told the BFB.

She was putting the BFB back into her bag, so they didn't see the Gigglers hiding behind one of the walls that the train was slowly passing.

Rover, Messi and the others had nearly finished running under Europe. They were under the Irish Sea now, very close to Dublin Airport.

Rover saw it first, because he was at the front, on Jimmy's crossbar.

'The light!' he shouted.

'Earthquakes!' shouted Messi.

Paddy O'Leary was looking for the can-opener.

Robbie had texted his parents. *Catch BFB at airport. She's in white plane. X.*

That was where Billie Jean and Mister Mack were now. Waiting for the BFB. So far, they'd seen twenty-two white planes landing. The BFB was on none of them.

Because she was on a train.

Actually, she wasn't on the train. Kayla had just got off, and the BFB was in Kayla's bag.

But she wasn't.

A little girl had seen the BFB's head sticking out of the bag while she was getting off the train with her dad. She thought it was the best doll she'd ever seen. It could smile and blink. So, when she stepped off the train, she grabbed it.

She lifted the BFB out of Kayla's bag.

'My dolly!'

Rover and the gang all ran and cycled out of the
tunnel and they were right beside the Dublin
Airport runway.

There was a white plane right in front of them.

'There it is!'

There was a white van driving away from the
plane.

'There *it* is!'

Paddy O'Leary found the can-opener. He put the
bread in the toaster. Then he went to the fridge
and took out the butter.

He left the fridge door open.

'Now is our chance,' said the evil green
vegetables at the bottom of the fridge.

The little girl's dad saw the little girl grab the
BFB.

'No, love,' he said. 'That's not your dolly.'

The little girl had pulled the BFB from Kayla's
bag and now her dad pulled the BFB from the
little girl's hands. But her grip was tight and

she wouldn't let go.

'*My* dolly!' she said.

Kayla turned just in time to see the BFB leave the little girl's hands, fly through her dad's hands, and head on up into the air. The little girl had let go suddenly and the dad's hands didn't hold tightly enough on to the BFB so she kept going up and up until she was right over everybody's heads.

Van or plane? Plane or van? Van or plane?

Where was the BFB?

Robbie saw his parents running up to the white plane – and that decided him.

'The van!' he shouted.

His parents would be checking the plane. So he'd go after the white van.

'Come on!'

'Tsunamis!' Messi shouted.

The poo was heavy. The poo was very, very heavy. But Messi hadn't forgotten why he was carrying it. And neither had Rover.

He got down off Jimmy's bike. He'd had his rest. He was ready to run again. And he didn't want the Gigglers to think that he was getting lazy.

They charged after the white van.

A middle-aged seagull called Sam was flying over the train station. His eyesight wasn't very good any more. In fact, he thought the train track below him was a river.

Then he saw the salmon. Leaping up, out of the river.

'Happy days,' said Sam. 'Fish and chips for the dinner.'

He swooped down and grabbed the pink salmon by one of its shoulders.

'Like, goop!' said the BFB.

The crispie twins' mam was coming home from her angry-yoga class. The Gigglers could hear her new green gym shoes on the path.

'How long have we got?' the biggest Giggler whispered.

'SIX SECONDS,' the tiny, tiny Giggler whispered back.

'And no poo,' the biggest Giggler whispered.

The white van had just gone past the train station. Rover, Messi, Miriam, Robbie and Jimmy were right behind it. They all saw the seagull.

'What's he got in his beak?'

'It's – ahhh!'

Sam the seagull had three thoughts as he tried to fly high above the station.

Here, in the correct order, are his thoughts:

1. This is the heaviest fish I have ever carried;
2. This fish's pink shoulder is padded;
3. Fish don't have shoulders.

Sam let go of the fish.

'Like, goop!' said the BFB.

Sam had a fourth thought.

'Why are girl babies always dressed up like salmon?' he wondered as he flew back towards the sea.

Paddy O'Leary's toast popped out of the toaster.

'Oh,' he said. 'I forgot all about the beans.'

The BFB was falling.

Fast.

The BFB was falling.

Faster.

No one was sure where she'd land or where they should stand to catch her.

But Messi did. He knew where – and he knew how.

But his tail didn't.

His tail was wagging.

The BFB was falling.

Messi's tail was wagging like mad. He was going to fall over.

'How far now?'

'THREE SECONDS.'

Messi was toppling.

The BFB was falling.

He thought of one more.

'Hurricanes!'

It was good – but not good enough. His tail slowed down but didn't stop. He had to stop it or his plan wouldn't work. He looked and saw the BFB coming straight down at him. He was wobbling. He couldn't get the bag off his back.

Then he thought of it.

The biggest mess of all.

'Life on earth!' he shouted.

His tail stood still and Messi got the big bag down off his back and on to the ground just as the BFB fell . . .

Right on to the bag.

'TWO SECONDS,' whispered the tiny, tiny Giggler.

'And still no—'

The BFB landed on cow, camel, goat, sheep, wildcat, rabbit, bat and mole . . .

'Poo,' said the biggest Giggler.

The bag didn't burst.

And the BFB didn't burst.

She bounced a metre back into the air, and into her mammy's arms.

'My baby!' cried Miriam.

'Like, goop,' said the BFB.

So.

If they hadn't run after the white van the second time, if Messi hadn't collected the poo, if Rover hadn't gone the wrong way – if, if, if, all the way back to the start of the story – Messi would not have been there at the exact right time to put the big poo bag in exactly the right spot to make the BFB bounce into the arms of her mammy.

Rover climbed over the Giggler's wall.

'Have you poo for us, Rover?' asked the biggest Giggler.

'Camel, cow or long-eared bat?' asked Rover.

'Oooh! Camel, please.'

'No sweat,' said Rover, and he climbed back over the wall. 'One lump or two?'

The twins' mam had stopped to look at all the excitement.

'Idiots,' she said.

And she walked on, straight into a big hill of the best camel poo in Ireland.

'Aaaah! My perfect shoes!'

The story was over—

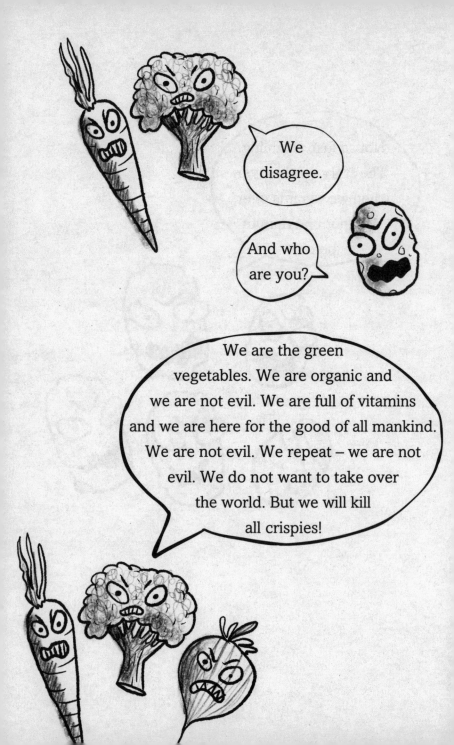

*

Paddy O'Leary picked up the can-opener. But then he saw that the lid of the can had a ring-pull.

'That's very handy,' said Paddy.

And he pulled back the lid.

The beans inside blinked.

And blinked.

Then they shouted.

'Watch out, people! The vegetables are evil!'

And the vegetables galloped back into the fridge and shut the door behind them.

The world was safe.

Saved by the beans!

And so, the story ends. The BFB had been returned to her parents ASAP.

But what does it mean?!

Sorry, we have to finish.

OH NO – they're back!

143

THE END

About the Author

Bestselling author Roddy Doyle is acclaimed across the world. He was born in Dublin in 1958 and still lives there today. He has won many awards for his writing, including the Booker Prize and a BAFTA for Best Screenplay.

He has also won the Irish Children's Book of the Year and was shortlisted for the prestigious CILIP Carnegie Medal. His novel *The Commitments* was turned into a blockbuster film directed by Alan Parker and opened as a musical in 2013 to rave reviews.

Rover and the Big Fat Baby is his eighth novel for children and the fourth book in the series which began with *The Giggler Treatment*.

About the Illustrator

Chris Judge is an illustrator, artist and children's picture-book author based in Dublin, Ireland.

His work is a mixture of illustration, painting and design, and his first picture book, *The Lonely Beast* (Andersen Press), won the 2011 Supersavers Irish Children's Book of the Year. He illustrates the Danger Is Everywhere series (Penguin) in collaboration with David O'Doherty, and illustrated Roddy Doyle's 2014 children's novel, *Brilliant.*

RODDY DOYLE

DOYLE

BRILLIANT

Gloria and Rayzer must save their Uncle Ben. The black dog has got him. That's what they heard their granny say anyway. And, she says, it's taken Dublin's funny bone too.

Gloria and Rayzer are really brave, but the black dog is scary and they can't fight it alone. Soon Dublin's children are helping . . . And then the animals in Dublin Zoo . . . And some cheeky seagulls as well. But could the biggest help of all be an ordinary word shouted – as loudly as possible – by all the kids together?